THE TRAITOR IS UNMASKED

EACH BETRAYAL BEGINS WITH TRUST

OVIYA R

Made with ♥ on the Notion Press Platform
www.notionpress.com

To this Universe

DISCLAIMER

Contents

Preface

Dear Reader,

You are special, for I am starting to write in the hope that this book will reach someone as special as you. Hope you have a good time reading this story.

May the Almighty above us, continue showering His blessings on all of us. My hearty thanks to all who have been my constant source of support and energy in the making of this book. A special mention to my proof readers for their time and efforts in the editing of this book.

Take few moments of your time to let me know what you felt about the book, so that I can strive harder to make you feel all the more special in my upcoming works. Also try out my other novels available on all online platforms. You can reach me through oviyarengesh@gmail.com.

Prologue

About the book

Adit, the young CEO is all set to move on to the next stage of his perfect life- marriage. Zarna, a budding ambitious psychologist, is all set to begin her career at DGI. Lyra, the entrepreneur, is all set to share her love with Adit. Anya is all hopeful to get her husband Nilesh back to his good health. It all seems perfect from the aerial view. But as we dive deeper, it is not.

Adit is struggling with a deep buried secret that pangs him day and night. Zarna faces a hit between her professional and personal morals. Lyra is forced to rethink her decision to marry Adit. Anya is eager to unveil her husband's past.

What happens when life decides to play merry go round with these people? Will the traitor be finally unmasked? Or is the traitor already waiting to be unmasked?

CHAPTER ONE

THE TRAITOR IS UNMASKED

Adit speaks

I snooze the alarm for the fifth time and turn to the other side of the bed. I suddenly feel droplets of sweat all over my neck and that forces me to open my eyes and look up at the ceiling. The air conditioner is off and the screens are open.

Any mother's usual technique of waking us up- my hindbrain reminds me of that and I revolt against that fact and continue to concentrate on my sleep by covering myself with a blanket.

Suddenly the fact hits me. The day is here- It is my engagement today; I realize and sit upright.

I grab my mobile from the table nearby and see that Lyra has sent me about ten messages in WhatsApp including an Audio message. There is a tag on Instagram too. I open Instagram on an impulse.

Lyra has posted our first picture together. The post was put up two hours ago. She has also captioned it beautifully- "The day is here, Adit??Lyra- From Friend to Fiancé. And I am the Boss of the CEO", She has also added some 'crying my heart out' emojis and hearts of different colours and shades. I like the message and read the last line again and feel glad that my mom is not on Instagram despite Veer compelling her to join. She would be pretty pissed off by that remark and will rethink my engagement with Lyra.

In the next half an hour I get ready in my usual attire for my typical day, a formal shirt, pants with an informal tie and head downstairs.

I see the house decorated with lights and diyas lit everywhere. I see the house packed with people, each busy in their own way.

Aunt Claire is busy setting her hair again and again. Chinki is asking everyone she sees to select one churidar among the three to wear. Uncle Dev is busy on the phone guiding the pandit on the route to our house. Unfortunately, I can't help but notice that out of the crowd gathered in my house today, only one or two faces have I seen during our downtimes.

My mother, Devaki is in her favourite place in the house- the kitchen finalizing the menu for the day. When the lady who brought ill luck to the family she married into, became the mother of the City's youngest CEO, she automatically attracted guests and friends. The fact of life.

My brother Veer is sitting on the corner sofa in the balcony with his laptop and headphones plugged into his ears. He is busy in his world of coding. I have been an inspiration to him right from childhood and when he completes his college the next year, he wants to become an entrepreneur just like me. But I can only pray to God that he doesn't end up doing the heinous act that I did to reach this place. I stand there as my mind takes my back to about five years from the present.

"Are you not ready yet?"

“Please don’t tell me you are going to the office today", My mother’s voice breaks my chain of thoughts and I get back to the present.

"You are there to take care of the preparations, ma. Why should I bother? You will always do the best for me. I have some meetings and agendas planned for the day. I will be back in the afternoon, much early for the engagement in the evening.", I cajole mom and head out.

The car is stuck in the usual city traffic on a typical weekday. So, I take out my mobile and go through the pending tasks and meetings ahead. I get a notification on top of the screen from our company’s socializing app. Another employee has committed suicide due to depression. This has been the third suicide in the past two months. The solution which I feel might set right these frequent suicides, will be there in place from today. I have discussed with the board members already and we are appointing a psychologist, who will be joining us today. She will be independent and will hear the concerns and grievances of employees. She is scheduled to join us today.

I lock my mobile screen and look out of the window. Having lost my father due to his untimely suicide, I feel the scars of it in my life till date. The least I can do for my company employees is to appoint a person who can help them. Today I am responsible for my life and I am shaping my destiny. But my mind wanders thinking what would have been my destiny if someone has stopped my father from committing suicide by offering him help.

Zarna speaks

I lift my head up from the table and glance at the mail for the fifth time, giving myself a false assurance that the contents of the mail would change in vain. I could vividly see stains of eyeliner in my hands from my eyelids as I leaned down with my head on the table.

I wash my face and hands and apply a light layer of eyeliner and stare at the contents of the screen again. I did not get a license to do psychotherapy yet again. This is the third time I am applying for it but somehow, I am not able to impress the jury with my presentation. I accept this fact and shake my head in a gesture of restarting my memory.

As my mom says I can't keep waiting for this license all my life. I have to move on and get myself some career to lead my life. I remind myself hopefully and get ready for joining the Devaki Group of Institutions (DGI). This is a huge opportunity for me to take my career to the next level.

"Breakfast is here at the table", the maid calls out as I go downstairs grabbing my mobile and car key. I head out after having my breakfast when there is a sudden downpour. I book a cab to avoid the risk of driving the car in this traffic and rain.

Lyra speaks

"And she always says that integrity and smart work has kept her at this level.........." I have gotten bored hearing my interview being played on YouTube all day.

Relatives have gathered for my engagement and mom can find no better opportunity to brag about her daughter. But I have to agree that I am not much of a family lifter or hard worker. I just had all sources and facilities and most importantly the support of my family to achieve in my career.

I graduated as the topper in Fashion Technology. I then started a firm that provided Fashion Consulting to Corporations. My first client was Devaki Fashions. Then there was a huge expansion in the business front and now I handle fashion consulting for three to four large corporations and I am also the Fashion Consultant for some of the elite groups in the city today.

"Hurry up Lyra, you need to start to the parlour now to reach the engagement venue on time", my mother cries out from the hall and I grab my mobile and bag when my eyes fall upon my mobile wallpaper. It is a selfie of us taken by Adit during our first unofficial date- to name it.

During our initial days at work, me and Adit used to get into a lot of silly arguments. But then, predominantly, there was a good understanding and friendship between us on the business front.

Adit's mother came up with the marriage proposal, days after he introduced me as his friend to all at his home. My initial reaction was shock as we did not see each other in that way.

Then, we had a formal date arranged by our parents to decide. We decided to visit the nearby park. I started the car and reached the end of the street when tiny droplets of rain made their way to the front glass of the car.

I continued driving in silence but made note from the corner of the eye that Adit also enjoyed rain in silence. There was nothing new that I wanted to ask Adit, so I just kept driving while my mind was analysing his character. I wanted to handle this as any other business proposal and my mind was working on the SWOT analysis of our life together. It seemed all the more viable.

When we neared the park there was a heavy downpour and we stared at each other on whether to get down or not.

As if to break our silence, "So no one told you life was gonna be this way..." The title song of the iconic sitcom F.R.I.E.N.D.S rang at once in both our mobiles and a broad smile escaped our lips. It was our parents on the call getting worried about us drenching in the rain and asking us to return. But we had other plans.

After half an hour of drenching in the rain, yes, we chose to return home because we had made up our minds regarding our marriage.

I can put it forth in the most cinematic way possible, but in reality, when I think of Adit, the first thing I feel is respect towards him before love. He is a man of principles and he has shouldered the family responsibilities at a very young age after the death of his father and he has taken his family to the next level due to his sheer hard work. His integrity was the first and foremost that made me consider the marriage proposal in the first place. All that I want is to be with him as a pillar of support come what may, and I expect the same from him. Dot.

Adit speaks

"....... The world is not the same as it was twenty years back. We all have to agree on the fact that we have a lot of pressure and stress engulfing us day by day. And when I say stress, it is not only on the work front but also in your personal front because your personal life is all the more important for this company.

We are not able to prevent suicides because we never recognise the mental pressure of an individual as a problem in the first place. When someone asks you 'How are you doing?', you respond for your physical health and for your other problems in life that are tangible. Never do we gather the courage to say I am emotionally exhausted or I am depressed. And when someone out of the blue gathers the courage to say so, he or she more often gets labelled as 'attention seeker' by this society.

Only when a life is lost, a wave of sympathy rushes all over. Then it falls back and settles down a week later, at the same pace it all started.

So, today, we want all of you to recognise that there is nothing wrong with feeling mentally suffocated at times. It is perfectly normal to seek help and share your problems.

I want our company to be a pioneer in maintaining a very good mental health of employees among other business aspects. Zarna is here to pave the way for that", I say and point towards Zarna.

I would believe her as a teacher rather than a psychologist. That too a teacher at the kindergarten would be apt. She gets up and thanks me with a formal namaste and waves to the employees gathered in the hall.

I continue my speech as I shift my gaze to the audience. "Lyra is available with us to share our problems. She will operate independently and has the ultimate right to make any changes to this organization that costs the mental health of the employees. I would like to end by reminding that the day we treat our physical and mental health at par, the world will become a peaceful place to live".

No sooner than I end the speech, the hall erupts with the thunder of applause from the employees. As I move from the podium to my seat on the stage, I can't help but feel self-satiated that the employees are clapping after understanding the true meaning of my words and not just for my face value.

"Your face value works magic. You indeed have a charismatic personality, Adit", Zarna's ironic words are feeble but soft and it drains behind the loud voice of the person reading the thanksgiving in the mic.

"Thanks Zarna. You are going to be the ray of hope to deliver the magic I ignited", I say, raising my decibel level beyond the sound from the speaker.

I spend the next two hours in the routine tasks and amidst that I spot Zarna taking a tour of the office at the corner of my eye.

"Quite an inquisitive lady", my personal secretary Sindhvi remarks and I nod.

When I start to go home later that afternoon, I meet Zarna again at the footsteps in the entrance of the office waiting impatiently.

"Hope you have covered the length and breadth of the office sprinkling positive vibes all around", I remark hoping she takes it as a joke.

"How can I forget the gardener of the office? I am waiting to spread positive vibes to the head man too", She smiled back. She got the joke and has decided to play along.

My car has arrived and I am right on time to reach my house for the engagement. But something stops me. I read the tension in her temples and probe.

"Should I drop you somewhere, Zarna?"

"Don't bother. I am trying to book a cab."

"It is lunch time already. You won't get a cab that easily for an hour or so. This is outskirts of the city"

She looks indecisive.

I open the car door signaling her to enter. "Give me the pleasure of dropping you home."

"Not home, to my HEAL Institute", She said more to the driver than to me and got into the car.

"I hope you don't expect to drop you every day."

"Hello! Usually I take my car. But I am not such a great driver and hence I prefer a cab on rainy days."

My mind nudges me to ask what HEAL Institute is. So, I ask casually, "Is HEAL institute your clinic?"

"Kind of. But it is a non-profit organization. I do consulting for mental health free of cost and it is up to my patients to contribute for my service as per their wish." She continues speaking about her life, patients etc.,

I nod silently and look at her serene face. I wish I had at least half the mental peace as her. But my dark past safely ensures that doesn't happen.

The journey continues with more of her talk about her career and my quiet reflection of my life to myself.

We reach the Institute in about half an hour.

Anya speaks

"Zarna will be here in ten minutes; we should be able to reach home earlier than usual." No response.

"Today we won't miss your favourite TV soap opera. We can then have an early dinner and then go to sleep." Again, no response.

Tears engulf and my voice nearly chokes.

Okay, I have not been speaking to Nilesh in expectation of some response from him. But I am never able to come to terms and speak more than three sentences straight into his eyes. Zarna says that I need to speak more casually with him and keep him involved in the happenings of the day.

I gather myself and try again, "We'll take a walk, love." I say pushing the wheelchair to the pavement and continue walking.

The weather is cool due to the morning rains and our walk is pleasant. The walk works wonders on his appearance. The breeze makes his tiny tangle of hairs on the front of his forehead wave slightly and the color of his face brightens.

One look at him, you would feel he is lively as ever. But after a brief five seconds you will realize he is still as a stone stuck to a wheelchair. Then I will have to explain to you that my husband Nilesh is paralysed and is in the initial stage of coma. I have got used to that by now. It has been nearly five years.

The veracity of the wind increases and I wrap my arms around me. Nilesh would also feel cold. I should cut down on my dinner for the next week and get him a muffler. That should keep him warm.

Suddenly out of no connection in particular, I feel thankful for having met Zarna. By no chance can we afford the treatment and counselling for Nilesh at the meagre income I get by doing household work. But she is treating him for free and taking care of all his expenses through her medical fund. She has also arranged for Nilesh's stay in the clinic during daytime and the nurses take care of him when I am off to work.

We continue walking when a car enters the entrance of the institute. It is not Zarna's car. We have been visiting Zarna for Nilesh's counselling for one and half years now that I can easily recognize her car.

The door opens and Zarna gets out with her usual smile waving to someone inside the car. She moves aside to greet another patient and just a millisecond before the car door closes, I happen to look at the person inside the car.

The door closes and I expect the car to leave but the car door opens again and the man inside looks at me with terror in his eyes. Not at me exactly, but at my husband. I can't be wrong. It must be Adit, my husband's friend from college. Just at the sight of him, I am reminded of a plethora of events dating back five years right from my love to my marriage with Nilesh. I get so engrossed in the past that I don't realize that Adit has come near us.

I shiver when he suddenly bends down near Nilesh and starts crying holding his hands. No response.

I stand there unsure on how to react and what to say.

"I am sorry", he keeps mumbling between his tears.

Zarna comes there with a perplexed look. "Do you know each other?"

Adit realizes Zarna's arrival and gets up wiping his tears.

"He is my college friend. He is that friend who means everything to you more than your family during your adolescent years until life drifts you apart." Adit speaks in a shaky voice and stops right in time. He adjusts his tie uneasily and clears his throat. This man knows to compose himself quite easily. Maybe men in general possess that talent I guess; I realize looking at Nilesh's face.

"How are you?" I ask, trying to avoid being left out.

Adit looks at me for the first time and I think he has recognised me, but he disposes of my question with a wave of his hand and shoots an arrow of questions at me.

"Why is he like this?"

"What happened to him?"

"Why are you both here?"

"Why the hell did he not contact me?"

"Why the hell are you silent?"

"She is waiting for you to give a break to your questions so that she can answer." Zarna responds on my behalf with a tinge of humour to it.

My honest answer would be this- 'So, you suddenly appear out of the blue, one random evening, throwing questions at me. You did not even care to pick his call during his tough times. You untied all ties with him one fine day when he was in trouble, and you want me to explain our very tough years in a single statement?' I keep these thoughts to myself and begin politely.

"You already know we were madly in love during college. The day before his final college project, I called him requesting that we marry soon before my parents end up marrying me to someone abroad. He came for me, leaving everything behind. We fought against both our parents and got married the next day. You would not know it because you would have been delivering your presentation then. I can completely understand why you could not attend our calls (This is a lie- he should have helped us. I can't forgive him for that, given that Nilesh has shared a lot about him and how much he means to him) That presentation took you to the next level and you got VC (Venture Capital) for your project that changed your life in the next few days. Our lives also changed for the worst. We struggled."

Adit stood silently as if taking in all the information. "Why is, why is he, why is he like this", he asked in a stammered voice.

"He wanted to meet you and discuss something with you. He said it was very important. He was coming to your house. On the way, he met with an accident. It was fatal. He was lucky that he escaped alive. And you are seeing the scars the accident gifted him. He was paralysed and he went into a partial coma. The doctors say that he is able to understand us but he is unable to react and he is under medication. There is no hopeful timeline that the doctors are able to give and I don't blame them. They are doing their best. Zarna is also doing us a lot out of her way for nothing."

"Don't take it that way. I get happiness and satisfaction. I wait for the day when he recovers to thank me. You can also wait till then, don't embarrass me." Zarna interrupts.

"Do you know what he wanted to talk to me about?" Adit asks and I nod in negative.

Is it my imagination or do I sense a feeling of relief on his face, I don't know.

Adit continues...

"I am so sorry for you and now that we have met, I can't make the same mistake of leaving him suffering like this. I can understand your financial position just by your look. I have known you since college. You had been the rich girl the whole college fancied about. Your current situation needs no explanation. Come and meet me at my office tomorrow. You can work there". That was an abrupt offer. But he got going before I could accept or deny whatsoever.

But someone else stops him.

"Are you alright? You look highly perturbed. Have some coffee and then leave. Why are you sweating on such a fine breezy evening?" Zarna asks in a genuine enquiring tone.

"I am fine", He says and continues walking to the car after rubbing the sweat from his forehead.

Lyra speaks

"He should be here in about ten minutes. He must be stuck in traffic." Aunt Devika says with her eyes intent on the door.

I have got tired waiting in the room and now I am in the hall joining the crew waiting for Adit. And the most difficult thing for a bride is to keep composed after your entire make over is done. My eyes fall upon the beautician whose biggest worry is whether she has to redo my makeup and I don't blame her. She meets my eye and signals me to keep calm and take deep breaths.

Suddenly there is a rush of sound coming from the guests and the parents. I can gather from the murmurs that Adit has arrived.

He walks inside silently with a grim face. He is surrounded by all the folks at the function, that I don't get to see him. Then he finally relieves himself and walks straight to his room. Straight to his room.

I know I am a practical business woman but that quite hurts when he walks across to his room without even casting a glance at me. But I nod my head dismissing my silly complaint. He is a CEO and he has a lot of things to worry about that are larger than his own engagement. Maybe.

Adit speaks

I tug the bed sheet tight transferring the anger straight from my brain to the poor bed. But the heart twitches in between giving a sharp pang of pain. Hundreds of thoughts are flooding my mind right now and my glared teary vision personifies my state of mind. I am unable to think clearly.

Just then by an impulse I took out a paper and pen. I start writing about that one mistake I have kept to myself these five years. As I keep writing, my vision and my mind clear like the clouds that wade away after a downpour.

It is actually Nilesh's solution for every problem that seems to go out of hand.

"Write it down. Keep on writing your version of the problem. Writing is a miracle by itself. It is not merely recording something in words. It is also getting something off your mind. That is why when you take notes during class instead of just listening you will feel that you have understood better. Actually, you place your confidence on the paper on which you have taken down notes that you can always get back to refer". He used to lecture like a philosophy professor and we used to tease him.

But the truth is, his technique has never failed me. Today is not an exception to that.

I complete writing, fold the letter and keep it in the drawer near the bed. This is the tenth time in the past five years I am writing my mistake down.

This is the perfect life I have been working for all these years and when it is all happening around me, I can't oppose myself. There is nothing I could have done about the past.

'Don't blame yourself for his state, Adit. It was a goddamn accident which has got nothing to do with you', I convince myself and start to get dressed.

As I go down in my light orange sherwani suit, all eyes are towards me, but my eyes fall upon Lyra, who is trying to avoid my gaze. The truth is, that I have forgotten about her in the last few hours. I need to make up for it now. I signal for Veer to come and whisper my plan in his ears and he nods in an understanding gesture.

The rituals start immediately and the race between our gazes continues throughout the ceremony.

Then the rings are given to us for exchange. She adorns her ring in my finger with a brief smile and I smile back. It is my turn now. I signal Veer and he runs knowing what to do.

All keep staring at me for about five seconds as I stand there with a clueless stare. Finally, the lights go off and there is a sudden pinkish limelight on Lyra and the light spreads to include me in the vicinity. Finally, Lyra's eyes meet mine.

I clear my throat and start speaking looking straight into Lyra's eyes.

"In my world, through all my darkness, my mother will be my sun and always you will be the star guiding me all along. Shall we orbit together?", I bend down on my knees and hold out the ring to her. Her flat lips curve into a smile with tears flooding her eyes. She shies as I slide the ring into her finger and there are cheers and shouts all around us.

I wink at Veer thankfully for saving the evening by switching off all the lights, focussing the limelight on Lyra at the right moment. The proudest person in the room is not, Lyra though. It is my mother. Thank God I didn't go as per my original plan of calling Lyra my Sun. I smile for the first time in the day, happy about myself. But the smile is brief for the pain finds its way back to my heart to haunt me.

Zarna speaks

Today I have decided to speak with him about this. I knock and enter his cabin. He is busy on his phone. He gestures to me to take a seat and continues speaking. As the talk progresses, I can see anger rising up in his words.

That is exactly what I want to speak to him about. It has been six weeks since I joined his office and he has always been a little upset or tense. Maybe he is a little off. Or it might be something that is bothering him. I am able to vividly read it from his eyes.

It is not a one-off incident that has brought me to his cabin today. I have noticed him a lot these six weeks. He eats at weird timings, his eyes portray clear lack of sleep, he shouts at his employees for silly reasons. Yesterday he shouted at an employee for changing the paper weight in his room. Can you imagine that?

I am sure something is bothering him. All I need to do is find out and do what I can to help. After all, what is the point if I work under him and he himself is not psychologically stable.

He would think that I am being over smart by accusing the boss under whom I work with by saying that he is mentally unstable but it is not my passing remark and I have no choice but to make him understand that.

Adit completes the call and looks at me with quizzical eyes and I start it as a casual conversation.

It has been fifteen minutes and finally, I have come to the point after dragging our conversation on unrelated stuff.

"Are you okay?"

"Yeah, just regular cold and cough", he says and fakes a cough.

"No, I am not asking if you are doing okay in the sense that the majority of people in the world enquire about each other. I am asking if you are mentally okay".

Adit shifts nervously in his chair and glances at his watch impatiently.

"Okay, is there anything specific you wanted to discuss? I am getting late for a meeting"

"Yes, this is important and it is about your mental health"

"I am doing good, if that's what you want to hear and If I require help, you know you will be the first person I will reach out to...."

I am not going to give up that soon.

"Were you like this right from your college days?"

I make a general remark but the phrase makes a strike with him as I see his eyeballs enlarge and his lips twitching. He tries to compose himself and says,

"Listen, I hope you know the responsibilities that I am shouldered with, at home combined with my marriage preparations. And I also hope you are educated enough to understand that being a CEO of a multinational corporation is not a cake walk. The rewards come with risks and the risks I take come with a toll on my mental health. Believe me it is more than the pressure you can solve by sitting face to face for a counselling session."

Okay that was harsh and a direct target at my profession which I didn't expect from Adit. Nevertheless, I need this job right now and I can't go beyond this.

I begin with a light smile, "Listen, I don't mean to say that......"

"May I come in, sir?" A tone that I recognise interrupts our conversation as both of us turn towards the door.

It is Anya. She enters the cabin with a file.

Adit stands up tense.

"Is everything alright?"

"Is Nilesh fine?"

I can get that he is concerned about Nilesh but he asks the question without facing Anya and looks distractedly around the room.

"Why do you ask that sir? He is good. I mean in the same state, no issues. I came here for your signature in a file." She says handing over the file.

Adit suddenly grabs the file, moves back uneasily and sits down on the chair. He grabs the pen and rushes to sign.

"The pen cap, Sir", Anya points out mildly and he says, "Oh sorry yeah yeah", he removes the cap and signs. I can see clearly that his hands are not steady.

He hands over the file back to Anya when the file drops accidently. All three of us try to collect the papers in the file. As we complete arranging the papers, I turn to see Adit at the door.

"I need to go. Have a nice day", he says remotely and leaves the cabin as the door closes.

"What has gotten into him? I mean I should not be saying this after all that he is doing to help me and Nilesh. But he is nowhere near to how Nilesh used to describe his character", Anya speaks more to herself than to me and leaves the cabin.

I am left at the cabin alone. I grab my mobile and get up to leave the room when my eyes fall on a photo on Adit's table. It is a photo of Adit and Nilesh from their college days. Nilesh looks more vibrant and youthful. Adit, I don't know, maybe he is happier in the picture or he is sober now. And most importantly, I don't remember the photo being here in this table when I met Adit in this room during my joining.

Adit speaks

My mother is at the door of my room for about half an hour now trying to check if I am okay. And I am at the bed staring at the ceiling wondering why Zarna confronted me like that at the office today.

"Are you sure you are alright?" My mother would not give up until I gave her a satisfying reply or lash out in anger. I wonder if all mothers are like that.

"Why do you insist maa? I am perfectly alright"

"For, right from the inception of your company, not even a single day have you been home this early. I am worried."

"I am also a human, not a machine. I need to take some time off to detox. And I have emotions too. Why the hell don't you all try and understand?" Okay I choose the second option of lashing out as I don't have a convincing answer.

I know very well that I am transferring my anger towards Zarna to mom and it is unfair. But don't we all do it? I know it is also not going to make me feel any better. But do I have a choice? No.

"More than a human, you are a son to me. The bonding of a mother and son is universal and not just to humans. I am there for you when you need me" she says and starts walking. I hear mom's faint footsteps becoming distant and distant as she goes towards her room. I can guess that she would be in tears now and I know for sure that I am the reason behind it.

She is right. She has always been my pillar of support and my world. But I am not the son she knows everything about. I have deep buried secrets. Secrets that would test her upbringing. Secrets that would break her heart forever.

Now coming back to Zarna, all this pressure today is because of her. I should keep her within the limits of an employee of the company. Today I would have blurted out everything if Anya hadn't interrupted us with a file. Zarna seems to be quite an investigator beyond a psychologist. She will soon connect the dots herself and she will come to me for the missing last thread.

Suddenly I am reminded of the letter I wrote on the engagement day and I rush to my side table and open the drawer with trembling hands. It is there folded, the same way as I kept it. Okay not so bad. My secret is safe with me. But no more do I need you to be so.

I tear the paper into pieces and I am about to throw it into the trash can when Veer barges into the room with a doubt in his project. I suddenly dump the pieces of paper back into the drawer and close it.

Half an hour later, Veer leaves the room with a contented smile after getting all his doubts clarified. But I am right back to my world of agony. I lie on my bed and close my eyes hoping to get some peaceful sleep this night unlike the nights in recent times.

Veer speaks

I finally managed to find a place to write my code in peace. Adit Anna's wedding ceremonies are starting tomorrow and the guests are here, well in advance for the wedding. My room is encroached already.

So, I finally settled in Adit's room. I know for certain that this room will not be taken over, thanks to my brother. He is very particular about people not invading his privacy.

My face breaks into a glee thinking of Lyra. Will Adit Anna be able to share his life and space with her? It is going to be fun. Okay now focus is on the project. I start to code my program in full swing.

I complete typing the codes and click on run and wait for what feels like an eternity. The code usually takes a huge amount of time to get executed. I pretend to see elsewhere other than the computer screen in the belief that the code would get executed quicker if I don't keep staring at it. But there is no response.

So, to divert myself, I start thinking about the application I am working on and how it could work wonders.

'If you tear out a paper by mistake or in anger and want to bring the contents back and retrieve the contents, my app comes to your rescue. You just need to place all the bits of paper together in any order and click a picture. My application will use its technology and comprehend the correct order of the pieces and will rearrange the bits of paper and create a single image of the sheet with correct content in the right order'. Unbelievable right? With this app, I am sure, I will get good placements. And who knows? I might also get nominated for the "Student of the year" award.

The "Realistic me", stops myself and I turn to the computer. I see the words, 'The program is executed successfully'. My app is finally ready for execution. I feel a rapid rush of adrenaline all over my body as I download the app on my mobile and my hands search for a paper to test my app.

I search around the room and finally reach out to the drawer of the side table beside the bed. My eyes land on the bits of paper crumpled and dumped in the drawer. I take it out as I hope it is not a paper from some boring agreement from Anna's office. I will get to know once I click the pictures and run the app.

I grab those pieces and place them on the bed. I then click pictures of the pieces of paper and click on run to get the writing on the paper in the right order. But it takes forever to run and I keep waiting impatiently when I hear my mom's voice seeking help to choose the decorations. I head downstairs leaving my mobile and laptop in the room. I forget about it as I get busy with the arrangements.

Anya speaks

"You have a visitor", the nurse at the clinic informed me and left.

I walk towards the garden pulling along Nilesh in his wheelchair. It is Adit.

"How are you?" He asks Nilesh as he bends beside the wheelchair.

"He is doing okay, thanks", I answer on his behalf and register my presence there. His glance shifts towards me as he stands up and clears his throat.

"I came here to invite both of you for my wedding. It is tomorrow. I want both of you to be there."

"Who is that lucky girl?"

"A business friend turned fiancé"

"We will be there"

Adit looks at Nilesh and stops speaking and I break the silence.

"Nilesh is feeling happy inside his heart but he is not able to express his happiness"

"If only he would......"

"No, doctors have confirmed that he could hear and sense everything around him but he is not able to react."

"And you and I can't predict his reaction on his behalf"

"But I am the love of his life. I know him, more than you did"

"I don't think so"

"Why do you say so?"

"If only I could tell you why? I mean there is more between two close friends and it is best to all if it remains as a secret. It will come to light if it is destined to be"

Adit looks at Nilesh sadly and starts moving. I can't be quiet any longer. I want to ask the question nagging in my mind all these years.

"One more thing...", I call out before I could stop myself.

"Yes?" Adit turns and walks back to me.

"Any idea what Nilesh wanted to talk to you about. That day when he was coming to meet you, the day of his accident...." I stop as grief chokes my throat. I wonder if I would ever accept that day of my life. The day when fate took over.

Adit turns with shock in his eyes.

"Did he mention anything to you?"

"Had he told me, I won't be asking you after all these years. But I know for sure that it was something important to both Nilesh and you. So, I thought to try my luck with you."

"I. I don't know. I, in fact, had no idea until you told me that he came for me that day. Maybe I will think it over."

Adit speaks hastily and walks towards the gate and I turn and look at Nilesh to find him staring at Adit with cold blood shot eyes. His gaze appears different to the look he usually has. I get a strong feeling that there is more to the story between these two friends that lies well hidden in their hearts and it is necessary for me to find it out.

Zarna speaks

I walk towards Adit's room with confusion in my mind.

I did not meet Adit after my confrontation with him the other day about his mental health. I just wanted to mind my own business and keep my career afloat. But I am now walking towards his room to talk on the same topic. But this time it is not voluntary, it is more of a compulsion.

When I got a call from Adit's mother Devaki, I came here all perplexed. But it all made sense when I reached here. Seems that some boomer relative has dropped this idea into her brain that I am a psychologist working for Adit and I can read minds and solve all the worries in the world. Hence, I was summoned to find out what was troubling Adit. Ridiculous.

But Devaki, the woman who personified peace and contentment was near to tears, all worried about her precious son.

"He is in his room. I want you to speak with him and find out what is troubling him so much. Please convince him to be cheerful at the function. The marriage ceremonies are going to start. What will Lyra think? Poor girl will be hurt if he ignores her like this. He cannot always make up like he did on his engagement. He was completely normal in the morning of his engagement day and evening when he returns back, we feel like we barely know him."

I can't help intervening there.

"Do you imply that he has been like this since his engagement?"

The day I joined the office is the same as his engagement day. This, I say to myself.

"Seems so. You see, Adit has changed a lot from college. All this pressure of the company has taken a toll on his character. He has been drifting from us as the company grew. But he has been recovering too, thanks to our constant love and thanks to Lyra. But again, on his engagement day something must have happened. He seems disturbed, I don't know what is bothering him."

"Just to be sure, does he have any medical complications?"

"He used to talk in his sleep. I am not sure if he continues it but I guess that has nothing to do with his stress."

Nowadays, people diagnose and decide the fatality of any illness all by themselves, thanks to the internet.

"Okay, I will try talking to him. But I am his employee and he has appointed me. I have my limits."

Devaki held my hands tightly as if bounding me in a promise. "For my sake, give it a try".

I nod and start walking towards the room. Not only my mother, all mothers around the world have their own way of getting things done.

I stop in my tracks as I hear Devaki speaking to Veer in the background, "If only that friend of your brother, Nilesh stayed with him, he would have been a better man. But your brother stopped contacting him all of a sudden when his college ended. They were more than close friends- just inseparable. Now we don't know where Nilesh is. Adit once mentioned that he has gone and I wonder where he would have gone?"

What? Were Adit and Nilesh that close. Why did they separate? And why did Adit hide from Devaki that he has met Nilesh?

Images of Nilesh and Anya flash before my eyes and I remember vividly how Adit had been behaving awkwardly when he saw Nilesh or Anya and it was not only my date of joining on the date of his engagement. It was also the day he met Nilesh and Anya after all these years.

Now I start walking to his room all determined to get the picture I have in my mind, painted clearly for me. I need to find out what Adit's stress and confusion has to do with Nilesh.

I enter or in fact barge into Adit's room hoping to find him sitting all alone frustrated but to my surprise, I find the room empty.

There is only a laptop and mobile in the bed along with some cramped pieces of paper. I gather and throw the bits of paper in the trash can and then close the laptop. I am this cleaning freak and a perfectionist. Habits die hard.

I am about to move out when the mobile on the bed starts ringing. I take the mobile on an impulse and see the name Jinesh appear on the screen. But before I could react, the call gets cut and I am left staring at the mobile screen.

I freeze and sit in silence as my mind tries to digest the contents of the letter on the mobile screen I just read.

Two hours later, I am at my house in my room replaying the words of the letter in my mind. After I read that letter, all I wanted was to get out of that house immediately. I had transferred the image of that letter to my mobile and deleted the image in that mobile. Then I rushed out.

Devaki being busy with the arrangements gave me the chance to sneak out of the house quietly. Even the thought of Adit makes me feel sick. There are hundreds of questions running in my mind right now. But nevertheless, I now know a secret which can change the lives of the people around me.

The notification sound from my screen diverts my attention and I look at my mobile.

It is an Email from the HR Team. I know what it must be even before I open the letter. My instinct is not wrong. It is my dismissal order from the Devaki group of Institutions. It must be the result of the conversation I had with him the other day in his cabin. And of course, Devaki would have told him about my arrival and even if Adit didn't meet me, he would not take a chance and tolerate my intervention. Given his buried past that I now know about, I don't expect him to do so.

I keep correlating my thoughts and the letter until I am tired. I close my eyes in an attempt to sleep.

Tomorrow is Adit's marriage. It is going to be a long day; I tell myself and beg my brain for some sleep in vain. I am left staring at the ceiling for hours until I sleep unconsciously.

Lyra speaks

"Now, for the final touch, the garland,", the beautician says and adorns the garland around my neck.

"The bride is all decked up"

"You are amazing"

"The prettiest Bride"

Comments flow in from my friends all at once but my eyes are focused on my mobile for his reply. In recent days, all my messages to Adit seem to go unnoticed. I know something is bothering Adit. If only he could trust me and share it with me.

More than that I also have a back thought in my mind which I negate to myself in every passing second. Whatever that is bothering him should not be in any way connected to our marriage. I don't want our marriage to be a coercive deal. It should be acknowledged and assented to by both of us.

Anyway, this is my big day and I should keep myself happy. I convince myself and break into a smile by looking at the 'all-decked up me' in the mirror.

"We are ready to go", the beautician says and I get up and walk to the stage after wearing a smile on my face. Adit is already on the stage. But he is not the Adit I was engaged with. He is clearly sleep deprived and his eyes are lost. As he sees me, his lips twitch into a brief smile. I am about to board the stage when I hear murmurs and voices behind me and I turn back to the audience.

"There is a marriage ceremony going on, we can discuss this privately." Adit's uncle is trying to stop three people who are walking straight towards the stage. I turn to look at Adit and he sits frozen with terror in his eyes as if he had been expecting them all these days and his fears have come true.

I turn to the men again. Dressed spick and span in formals, I think they must be government officials. I am not wrong.

They take the lead wasting no time.

"We are from the office of the Registrar of Copyrights. I am the senior registrar. He is the Assistant Registrar and he is the Sub-Inspector of the local station." He introduces himself and the two men near him.

"This can wait but not the auspicious time. Can we talk about this later?", Devaki intervenes.

"I am afraid not. I have received a complaint against Mr Adit regarding Copyright Infringement and we need to take him for interrogation."

"What is this about and who registered the complaint?", It was Veer, Adit's brother.

"I gave the complaint and I have proof". A young woman enters the hall with a print out in her hand.

"Zarna!!!!!"Adit shouts and gets up from the wooden ceremonial plank.

I cannot tolerate this anymore. I go to her and grab the paper from her hands and look at it. It seems like a crumpled paper that has been stuck together using some software. The process of how the letter came is not bothering me now. I am bothered about the contents of the letter.

I start reading the letter to myself and as I digest the contents of the letter, my head starts swirling.

The letter reads as follows,

"Dear Nilesh, I can't believe I am back again. Writing down my sin to you and addressing it to you. I know very well that this letter would go to trash. But I am writing this to feel better and to breathe some fresh air and come out of the pollution in my mind. Where do I start and what do I tell? The same story again. But this time the story also has the aftermath. I met you today. I thought I had to face confrontation from you, but I had to offer consolation. The live charismatic Nilesh I knew of, is now staring at this world with blank eyes day and night.

Nilesh, every time, I wrote down my secret, I used to think, if only I could tell you everything as easily, I would write it down. But today I realized that even If I gathered the courage to tell you, you are not in the state to listen. I badly want to blurt out everything to Anya but I just can't.

Now you have to understand that I am not just Adit, your friend from college. I have a dependent mother and brother. There is Lyra, and there is my company, which is the kingdom I have built with all my blood and sweat. I can't let go of all this easily. It is all my years and years of hard work.

The only sin I did was to steal the identity of the code. Do you remember that night, Nilesh? We were so frustrated that we were not able to complete the coding for our project and we were getting errors.

You were so stubborn not to give up because we had Venture Capitalists (VC) coming up the next day along with our project viva. We wanted to present our project to the VC and get it financed. Given our financial backgrounds, getting VC funding would change both of our lives forever. We both knew that very well. Starting a new start-up had been our dream right from our childhood and we were struggling for that.

After some point, I gave up and went to sleep but you insisted on trying and I left it to you and slept.

The next morning, I woke up and saw the project done. You had completed coding our idea and that gave us the breakthrough we needed for our new business venture. My joy then knew no bounds. But you were missing. I just found your note saying Anya is in danger and you need to hurry and you will be back. Believe me I was waiting for you. But practically speaking, I cannot miss the viva for you. I did the realistic thing.

Our idea rocked in the viva and I was asked to present to the VCs. Again, I had to do the realistic thing because there was no sign of you. Let us agree here that had you been in my place, you would have done the same thing.

The VCs were happy with our project and they were ready to fund it immediately and I had to sign and close the deal. I could not have waited for you and lost the opportunity. But do you remember the endless nights we spent talking about how difficult it is to acquire VC support? I signed it and took the entire credit for that idea and code. That deal changed my life for good.

I know you won't believe that I am crying now but I am. I am truly sorry for you. Seeing you in that state turned my guilt to pain. But there is nothing any of us could have done about your accident. It was fate.

Till I met you today, I thought you were angry at me for betraying you, for stealing your efforts and taking credit for it. I thought you stayed away from me for the sake of our friendship. I didn't pick your calls because I was afraid of facing you. But Anya tells me that you came to see me. You must have come to confront me and claim what is rightfully yours and today I am the one to be blamed for your state.

I agree that I was selfish to not trace you all these years. But all this new name and fame took me deep down beyond our friendship and college days. Words cannot express the regret I feel today but nevertheless that doesn't make me any less of a traitor. I can only hope to atone for my sin when you get back to your conscience and I will carry the burden with me till then because none other than you might understand this. I promise you that I won't let you suffer for money any longer.

-Yours treacherously, Adit."

As I complete reading the letter, I see Adit's signature at the bottom and I sink into a nearby chair with tears nearly flooding my eyes.

Someone grabs the letter from me and I look up to find a young lady in plain saree and a motionless man in a wheelchair near her. There dies my only hope that all this could be fabricated.

The letter then goes for circulation across the hall and there are whispers that escape amidst the silence in the hall.

As the officers start their proceedings, the whispers become more evident as words float across the marriage hall. Everyone is shocked! Adit, who had been the epitome of perfection has fallen to grave right in front of their eyes.

I turn to look at Adit who keeps his eyes transfixed on Zarna looking for an explanation. Suddenly, the man who I admired for his hard work and integrity now appears to be smeared full of treachery and sin.

Now it is Zarna's turn,

"I didn't imagine you to be such a blood sucker who can do anything for his name and fame. I found this letter as an image in a mobile in your room and I couldn't keep quiet after knowing all this. It is of no use trying to confront you, so I decided to confront those who love you."

"Anna!!! The only inspiration in my world is you and I always wanted to be like you. Today I want to be nothing like you. How could you betray Nilesh Anna? Even after seeing his state, you did not break. I must have gathered your torn letter to test my app and see if it could comprehend the torn letter. I left the code running and went downstairs to help mom and I forgot all about the letter. Zarna must have seen it then. But today I feel happy for creating the app so that you were exposed."- It was Veer.

There are sudden murmurs around us and I could hear voices around me,

"Water! water!",

"She has fainted"

"Call the doctor"

On one side, Devaki aunty has fainted and on the other side, the officials are dragging Adit. I am aware of all this happening around me but I just sit there motionless.

My parents nudge me to intervene and save Adit but I turn and see Anya. The lady has been standing by her paralysed husband all these years and I suddenly felt her pain in my heart.

I have chosen the wrong person, the man who has been living his friend's fortune all these years. It is my fault. The traitor has to be unmasked one day and it has happened. The deal is cancelled.

Gathering all my strength I walk straight to the car ignoring everybody. I need to be alone.

Zarna speaks

I am sitting in the corridor of my clinic when I see Anya coming towards me. It has been about six months since Adit was arrested on copyright charges. The case has been going on in full swing.

"The judgement will be delivered today ", Anya says with a short smile on her face.

"Good. There is light on the other side waiting for you."

"Light, that was kept away from me and you ignited it for me and till date, you continue to support me for the legal fees."

"Come on! Millions and millions earned by Adit are all the result of your husband's idea, his code and you are a millionaire in guise. And I need my money back with interest." I joke trying to cheer her up.

"What would I do if it were not for you? I may not be able to thank you enough, but I want you to know that I will always be for you when you need me" Anya says and gives me a brief hug.

"Okay, I guess you must get going, the hearing will begin in an hour."

"Yes, I am just starting. I want to be there when the judgement is delivered. I don't want to take the risk of Nilesh getting infected by taking him there. So, I prefer he stays at the clinic. The nurse told she will take care of him."

"Yeah, it seems right."

She starts walking away from me and I can see the image of Adit being dragged from the marriage hall before my eyes.

The day Adit got arrested, I was so relieved and I strongly believed that I did the right thing. But I am still not able to get over the look I saw in Adit's eyes when he was dragged by the officials. I could not comprehend the emotion, but I felt empathetic for him. I still have a nagging feeling that I did not do the right thing and I am not able to get over it. After all, it was Adit's own confession and he has agreed to everything even in the court. What could go wrong in this? But something is still amiss. If only Nilesh could speak!

I open my mobile to check my next appointment for the day when I see a new E-Mail in my inbox. It is the mail I have been waiting for all these years and there is happiness all over my face. I have received approval to conduct a psychotherapy test in my clinic with adequate precautions. But there is a condition. I am fully responsible for the risks involved and the results of the test are confidential and it still remains void for all legal purposes.

I look up from my mobile and find a familiar figure walking towards me. I have an unexpected visitor. And now, all of a sudden, I know the right thing to do.

Lyra speaks

I am outside the court. I offered to stay in the car and I could see Zarna and Anya talking in the distance. I just hope we are not late to do the right thing.

On the pavement outside the courtroom, I could see Devaki aunty and Veer conversing with each other. Devaki aunty has changed so much comparing to her look on the day, my marriage with Adit was planned for. She is wearing a plain saree and her eyes are weak and overloaded with tears. Veer is sitting nearby comforting her. But gathering from whatever he spoke to Adit, that day, he is pretty much pissed off at his brother. In fact, we all were.

After their talk, Zarna and Anya walk to the courtroom and I think Zarna must have explained everything to Anya and I believe that Anya would do the right thing.

I sit there and replay Nilesh's words in my mind. Yes, Nilesh's words at the clinic just an hour back.

Zarna was surprised to see me at the clinic this morning. Zarna and myself had a short talk about Adit and Nilesh and both of us strongly felt that something was amiss. So, we decided to attempt a psychotherapy test on Nilesh to make him speak.

As Zarna tells me, through a form of psychotherapy, you can inject drugs on an individual and make him speak out what is in the deep of his or her mind. It is a form of treatment to relieve one of the stress or depression deep rooted in their minds by making them speak it out.

We were reluctant at first to do it without Anya's permission. But time was running out and we decided to go ahead.

Though Nilesh did not cooperate too well for the analysis, we finally heard him speak. His voice was coarse and dry but his words were clear and he was speaking right from his conscience with no reaction or emotion.

We asked him only one question, "What happened on the night when you were at the final stage of the project with Adit?"

His words were full of stumbles and breaks but nevertheless clear and stubborn.

"Traitor, unforgivable, stole the code, He slept off."

Hearing those fragments of speech from Nilesh, I felt shattered and turned to leave but when I heard his full statement, I stopped in my tracks.

"It was his code. It was his code."

Zarna intervened, "What do you mean?"

"Adit slept, he was talking in his sleep. He gave the solution for the right code in his sleep. I heard it, I coded it, could not tell him, Anya is waiting for me at the bus stop, I need to go, Adit feels guilty, I will speak, I want to speak."

Between the broken words, we got the message. It was Adit's code and idea after all and he is not a traitor. I guess Adit himself doesn't know that it is his idea- the idea that transformed his life.

Nilesh was unconscious and back to his paralytic state once we stopped our testing. Zarna is hopeful that she will be able to make Nilesh recover by harnessing the power of psychotherapy.

But his words, though short, changed everything around us. So, Adit has discovered his idea in his sleep. He had put his body and soul in the idea all these years. And sadly, he was named a traitor. At that moment, I loved Adit more than ever.

Zarna and myself wasted no time and we headed to the court to reveal the truth to Anya and make her withdraw the complaint on Adit.

We had only one option- To speak and convince her to withdraw the complaint out of the court because the psychotherapy test will not be considered as evidence in the court of law.

I see people and press rushing towards the door of the courtroom and I turn in that direction. There he is- Adit. The CEO I fell in love with now looks like a commoner with a faded T-Shirt and shabby pants. But let me tell you the irony. I want him more now. Devaki and Veer run to hug him and I see all of them happy.

My eyes land on Anya. She frees herself from the crowd and tries to get into an autorickshaw when all cameras surround her.

She remarks with a shaky voice without waiting for their questions, "There is no secret that time doesn't reveal. And the traitor is not always masked. He can be near you all unmasked and you never know who the traitor is. This is what makes life interesting." She says and walks away without turning back. Must have been very hard for her to accept the truth.

I now divert my attention to Adit and he is now talking with Zarna. As they speak, Adit turns at me and starts walking towards me. Seeing his calm face, I feel glad for doing the right thing at the right time. I used my contacts at a high level to get the psychotherapy test facility approved for Zarna. That brought the truth to light. That saved Adit, that saved my Adit.

Adit speaks

For the first time in my life, I look at Lyra differently. Every night at the prison, her indifferent face at the marriage hall when the officials dragged me flashed before my eyes to haunt me. But today, in her solid black kurta sitting in her car, she ironically personifies an angel flying towards me. Her eyes are glowing with happiness and pride, the same expression I saw in her when she agreed to marry me.

She gets down from the car when she sees me and smiles at me. I hug her on an impulse- our first hug and tears roll down all over my face before I could gather my emotions. We move apart and she casts a sympathetic yet longing look at me.

I ask the question that has been nagging me. "How did you believe in me?"

She smiled and replied.

"Boss, I do my study carefully before accepting or cancelling a business deal. Do you think I will let you go that easily if it is my life that is at stake? During our initial days at work, I have seen the hard work and talent in you. Somewhere that did not tally with the blame imposed on you. You could not have raised the company to this level if you were just a traitor living with your friend's idea. My SWOT analysis went wary. I wanted to somehow hear it from Nilesh before letting you go. And that's what I did."

Before I could thank her, the reporters surround us and for the first time, I feel confident to face the public. After all these years, I want to talk about Nilesh with someone other than me. I grab the mic and start speaking.

"Nilesh and myself have always been in this idea together and it is unfair to give the credit to one of us. All this business belongs to both of us. I am making Anya as an equal shareholder in all my business and she will manage it on behalf of Nilesh and let us all pray for Nilesh's speedy recovery to being his own self.", I register my words strongly with the Press and walk towards the car with Lyra by my side.

I stop when I spot Zarna speaking with mom and Veer. I can find ways to thank Lyra and make it up for the rest of life. But it is different in the case of Zarna. She has gone out of her way to help me. She must have had at least a little amount of trust left in me when I myself strongly believed that I was a traitor.

I have a lot to tell her and thank her, but now I want to say something that would make her glad. "Zarna, I cannot thank you enough. But firstly, consider me your best patient whose mental health you have restored back at its best. And let us meet at the office tomorrow. The company needs you. We all need you there. But no longer as my employee. I am planning to fund the expansion of your clinic. You can work there independently for the betterment of the mental health of my company's employees," I say and move towards our car with Lyra leaving a smiling Zarna behind.

As I continue walking, I realize that I am wearing a smile after a long time. And you want to know the best thing? After years, I don't feel like I am wearing it, I am feeling it.

.....THANKS FOR YOUR TIME.....

9 798889 092919

Printed by Libri Plureos GmbH in Hamburg, Germany